Pack Present

By Huckleberry Rahr

ISBN eBook: 978-1-959981-49-7
ISBN paperback: 978-1-959981-50-3

Editor: Weslee Imrisek
Developmental Editor: Angela Grimes
Cover Art: Getcovers.com
Formatting: Huckleberry Rahr

Chapter 1 - Enemies to Lovers
Jade

"Bevin, hurry up! I don't want to be late."

Bevin's eyes cut over to me. "Jade, as bad as traffic can get, it won't take us that long to drive from Stanford up to Were House. We'll be home in just over an hour. They won't have dinner without us." The citrusy scent of his amusement filled the car. "As excited as you are to eat, I'm looking forward to wrapping my husband in my arms."

Cutting my eyes to him, I grumbled, "Look, buddy. I'm the one who has your *and your husband's* pups in my belly. Traffic sucks even more when pregnant. Each minute feels like, I don't know, five? Ten? A year?"

As the first gay alphas, Bevin and José really wanted a family to continue their legacy. When they'd asked me to be part of their journey, how could I say anything but "yes?" Even though werewolves could tell a lot about other people, and Bevin loved information, he had a blind spot when it came to my pregnancy.

Last spring, Bevin, José, and I started artificial insemination. We were all thrilled with how quickly it took. The kids would all be mine, but they wanted the father, or fathers, to be up to chance.

Because of who I was, and my animals, I had a pretty good idea about the fathers, but by agreement, I hadn't told them ... either of them.

A scowl crossed over Bevin's face before it was replaced with a warm smile. "First off, stop with the information about how many babies you're carrying. You know I don't want to know! And, second, would ice cream help?" He waggled his eyebrows at me, as if he didn't know the answer before he asked.

I crossed my arms and slumped. "Yes," I said with a pout.

"It always does." He smirked.

We'd returned to Stanford, our stomping grounds for post graduate studies, to sit on an end-of-semester panel to talk about the process of going from undergrad student to professionals and the medical studies in between. Now that we'd finished our residency as medical doctors, it was nice to give back when we had time.

We stopped at our favorite sweet shop off campus and then hit the road. I focused on licking my malt amore, taking my life in my hands as Bevin drove. He wasn't the worst driver in the world, but everyone needed a weakness, and driving was his. But with my low energy and aching feet, we both agreed he should take the wheel.

Bevin merged into traffic, and my head throbbed. *Gods above! Traffic is awful this time of day!*

Moving five miles per hour on the interstate, Bevin let out a sigh. "Did you finish your Christmas shopping?"

I glared at him. "You know I haven't. I hate shopping, and with this belly ... gah! It sucks. January seventeenth can't come soon enough."

"Why don't you go out with—"

"If we go out together, how do I get her a gift? You know, as hard as it was to be single, at least then I didn't have to come up with gifts ... and she's impossible."

"I've been dealing with this with José for years. Maybe we can go out on our next day off." The car jerked forward as traffic lurched onward.

"You mean in April?"

He laughed. "Something like that. Though, you'll get some time off once the kiddos come."

I rubbed my protruding stomach. "They can't come soon enough. I try to make deals with them, you know. But they're as stubborn as their fathers."

Bevin rolled his eyes. "They aren't due until January. What type of deals are you making with my kid?"

"Kids, bucko. I told you, there's more than one."

He shook his head. "And I told you, no details, Mama. You and José have details. You two want to know everything. I don't. I like surprises."

Everything ahead of us sped up, and I could almost taste Oscar's dinner. Maybe he'd make a chicken pot pie, or lasagna, or pasta with meatballs and garlic bread. My stomach growled as I imagined all the possibilities. "Why is that again? How is information a bad thing?"

"Just don't tell me. More than one, fine. Good. But I don't want to know if the kids are mine or José's until they are born. And I realize you can tell if they'll be wereanimals. I don't want to know that either." His voice rang with finality.

"Or shifters."

Shifters were a separate kind of animal-human hybrid. Growing up, I thought there were only werewolves. That was until I was bitten by a werepanther. A few years into college, Bevin and I were recruited by a small, secret, government agency—one that knew about werewolves—, the SSLD. They also knew about a small group of bird shifters. Thanks to a half-wit nurse—well ... a competent soldier, just no one who should've been working with needles—I ended up being injected with a serum that gave me the ability to shift into a black swan.

"Having two wereanimals prowling within me, and my swan, any child of mine has the potential for their own menagerie, you know." Half in my own thoughts, I hadn't realized I'd said the last aloud.

"Oh, my gods, Jade, I'm going to kick you out of this car, here and now." The cinnamon scent of annoyance exuded from him.

I smiled wide as I finished the last bite of my cone. "Nah, you wouldn't risk hurting our kids. But, no, I won't tell anyone but the kiddos themselves if they're full-blown human, or wereanimal."

"You haven't told anyone?"

"Who would I tell?"

He gave me a disappointed look. "José and I don't keep any secrets. You're telling me, you two do?"

With a huff, I narrowed my eyes at him, about the only offense I had. "Either we change the subject, or I start giving you specifics."

He snarled. It could've been at the traffic, which had jammed up again, but I doubted it.

Time to change the subject. "Okay, what did you get José?"

He slumped. "Like I said, he's impossible to shop for. Do you have any ideas?"

I laughed, relaxing back in my seat. "I knew it! You're no better than me."

"Never said I was. Spending all our time at the hospital doesn't translate to much time to do anything else."

"Don't forget our part-time job at the SSLD. I mean, I don't remember the last instance when Owen dragged us in, but I *think* we're technically still on the payroll."

"I went in a couple of weeks ago. You didn't join me."

I narrowed my eyes. "Really? Why not?"

"You said something about sleep and murder."

Thinking back on that day, I laughed. "Oh, yeah, I remember. Well, one day I'll get back to that compound. Maybe after the kiddos are walking."

Bevin laughed. We spent the rest of the drive discussing possible Christmas gifts.

When we finally arrived at Were House, Oscar hadn't prepared dinner; José had. Tacos—beef, pork, chicken, vegetarian, and shrimp. He made sides of rice, beans, and salad. The food smelled and looked fantastic.

As I made my way past the living room to the dining room, I stumbled. My belly hit a side table and knocked down a lamp. Milo, who sat on a couch, chuckled. "Got it. When you finally pop, will you become less klutzy again?"

Laughter came from everyone present. Owen, my brother, sat in the dining room with his wife and my best friend, Sarah. Bevin had made it to the kitchen to hug his husband, José. Alex and Quinn, two other packmates, sat with Milo in the living room. I wasn't sure where everyone else from the pack was, but if they'd heard Milo, I'm sure they'd be just as amused.

From the kitchen, José snorted. "You think Jade was ever anything but a klutz? You've known her long enough to know this about her. She can trip over a speck of dust."

I rolled my eyes, "Really, José? Where's the love? Where's the respect? I'm carrying your children. Don't I get something for that?" As I glared in his direction, I almost toppled over.

From the dining room, Owen leapt up and caught me, barking out a laugh. "That's my sister. But let's not hurt my future nieces and/or nephews."

From the kitchen, Bevin snarled. "Enough! I don't care who knows what. Until the babies are born, no more talk. I will make it an alpha law if I have to."

The laughter started up again at his ire.

I made it to the dining room without stumbling again. A furry beast dashed out and leapt into my lap. Brooke came out from the hallway which led to the bedrooms and sat next to me. She eyed the black cat and sighed. "That thing is obsessed. Where are her brothers?"

Milo waved. "Over here. Annabelle may love Jade, but Enoch and Red love me."

Brooke narrowed her eyes at them, then turned to face me. "Remind me how these beasts—who shouldn't like any of us werewolves—got their names, and then I'll answer your question from last night about why no one trusts you to name the babies."

Oscar placed a mug of herbal tea in front of me, and I sighed. I wanted coffee more than I wanted to admit. "It comes from one of my favorite book series' that starts with *Wyldling Snare*. This black beauty is named after the heroine who can do a type of magic with water. The fact that she loves to swim is just proof that all black felines are beautiful—"

"And crazy?" Brook cut in.

I huffed out a sigh. "Maybe."

Sarah chuckled. "I can't say she's wrong."

"Anyway," I continued. "The white one is named after the male main character, the silver knight."

Sarah shook her head. "Okay, but why is the calico cat named Red? I've read the book. Excellent, I agree. But I don't see it."

"Really? Red has an orange circle around one of his eyes like the monocle Red uses in the books."

It was too much for Sarah, who laughed. "Why have I never noticed that?"

Owen leaned over and kissed her. "Because, love. Like a smart werepanther, you avoid the cats that shouldn't like us."

She nodded. "You're not wrong. They like the werewolf alphas—as if they know who the leaders are—Jade, and Milo. Besides that, they just tolerate everyone else in the house."

"No, they love Raquel," Bevin said, with a snort.

I thought about our resident drag queen and couldn't imagine anyone, person or animal, not loving her. "Of course, they do. It's Raquel."

José brought in the platter of food, and the table started to fill with the pack members. Over the years, the pack had grown. Not everyone ate together, though everyone was welcome. The bigger apartments had their own kitchens, and some people preferred to eat as a smaller family unit. Some went to town to eat. Some would come through and eat later. That being said, many people joined us, enjoying the time to reconnect and eat amazing food.

The last to join the group was Violet, the security director, who worked and lived in the basement. As an introvert, she didn't often socialize with the pack. Her one time to reconnect was the meals.

She passed the dining room and walked to the living room. Milo stood, and the two embraced. It had taken a while for Milo to get over their apprehension about wolves. By the time they had, I had moved on. I realized I deserved someone who loved me for me. All of me.

But, as was my habit, I brought Violet to the Youth Outreach Center when she asked about programs to help her find a community. Whereas she didn't find a community, she did find Milo. Milo, for their part, came to understand and trust the wolves.

My relationship with them blossomed into a deeper friendship even as they discovered love with Violet.

Seated beside me, Brooke squeezed my leg. "You okay? Your emotions are a bit crazier than normal, Ms. Preggo."

I leaned into her, taking the strength she offered. "Better now." I whimpered. "I have to go shopping next week."

She laughed. "Poor baby. Sarah and I can help you, and you know it. Now, eat before you faint dead away or whine all night about fainting."

I kissed her cheek and leaned back in my chair. My plate, as always, was already full of food.

Chapter 2 - Birds of a Feather
Jade

My back hurt. After all, a full soccer team was using my spine as their practice kicking bag.

Every morning when I woke up, I was in agony. I groaned as I tried to move, but the weight of the babies held me down.

Strong hands massaged my back, and I moaned in pleasure. "Gods above, marry me."

"You know, if you didn't say that exact same thing, in that exact same way, to your chocolate shake, I may take you seriously." Though she teased me, she didn't stop.

After a few moments, I rolled to my back and looked up into the dark eyes of the last person I'd ever expected to fall in love with. Brooke Winter. I wasn't even sure how it had happened. After the battle with the San Mateo wolves, I had nightmares. She was the only one who could help keep me calm, the only one all my animals trusted.

That was the first piece of the puzzle. Then I realized she was the one who always put flowers in my room when I came home for a weekend with Bevin. She gave me trinkets, in the name of being properly dressed when we all went out. Sometimes I was slow, but it occurred to me, she went above and beyond all the time, making sure to find items I'd appreciate. And every time my emotions ran wild, she texted or called, checking up on me.

It was more than her role as a submissive wolf in the pack. I knew that when Bevin's grandfather died, and she didn't immediately call him. I spent time with him grieving until he and José could catch a plane to Wisconsin. She did call and help him, but it took a few hours. She never let my emotions run with me for that long.

I reached up and cupped her cheek. "How can you be so pretty in the morning?"

"Oh, shut up and get dressed." She shook her head with a tiny smirk.

Smiling, I did as I was told.

In the dining room, I found oatmeal and tea. I wasn't scheduled for work, though Bevin was. I watched as people came in and out, grabbing something quick and heading off to their jobs.

When Oscar started cleaning up, I sighed. "I want to take a walk into town, maybe get hot chocolate or an ice cream cone. I just don't know if I can make it all the way in and back in my condition."

"Child, look at you. You're the size of a house—not this monstrosity of a house, but a regular one. You can barely make it from one side to the next. There's no way you're making it to town. You have the day off, relax."

Across from me, José smirked. "It's nice when I don't have to be the voice of reason. You know, the mean one. I agree with Oscar."

"I could walk for a bit, and then you could drive me back."

He got up and walked around the table, kissing my forehead. "I would if I didn't need to get to work. I have a meeting this morning. If I didn't, I'd take the day off to play."

Violet ran up from the basement. Oscar threw a protein bar at her, and José trotted after her. He was the big alpha around the house, but she had seniority over him at their office.

Once the door shut, I trudged to the living room and dropped into the recliner I'd adopted as my nest. Immediately, all three cats piled around me. Annabelle and Enoch curled on my belly, Red taking sentry at the top of the chair.

Several years ago, the pack was doing a training session. Owen decided to have the wolves search for the panthers—it had been a while, and they needed the practice. Trying to be clever, I crouched down in some bushes, blending in with the shadows. Sarah and I usually hid high in the treetops.

It didn't take long for what felt like hypodermic needles to stab me in my hind quarters. A mad dash back to Were House determined that three kittens had adopted me as their own. Within minutes they'd adopted the pack as well, winning over Bevin and José almost immediately.

The pack searched for other owners who may have lost the kittens, but after a month decided they were homeless and now truly part of our pack. Despite being the smallest beasts in the house, they strutted about like they owned the place.

Alex sauntered in and sat on the couch across from me. "Morning, sunshine."

I tilted my head. "Don't you have work?"

"I'm working Saturday this week, so I have today off. Why? Bored? A day off and you can't stand it?"

I snorted. "Maybe. I was thinking of taking a run, but the idea of going furry with my belly this big, it's just too much. But I could become Swan. I can fly like this, it's barely anything in my bird form. I just need to do something active. This sitting around all day is driving me batty."

"Well, if you do decide to take wing, would you be mad if I check with Bev first and maybe monitor while you're out there?"

"Gods! You're my babysitter, aren't you?" I threw my hands out to the side in frustration. "I'm going to kill them in their sleep. Tell Bev that. I know where he sleeps and if he doesn't watch out, he won't wake up."

Though the words brought a flash of an old nightmare, I stuck to my guns and glared at Alex. They were as culpable as the others.

They held up their hands. "Fine, sorry. I won't ask permission, but can I still sit in the backyard and watch? It isn't as much about monitoring as enjoying the show. You as a swan are beautiful."

"Versus me as a whale, which is getting unbearable." I massaged my belly, which felt like it'd grown even bigger overnight.

One of Alex's eyebrows rose. "I will report this to Brooke. She still scares me but watching her take her ire out on you is kind of fun."

Sighing, I slumped. "Fine, whatever. Let's do this. I need to move."

We passed by the kitchen where Oscar hummed while he worked. "I'll have lunch ready when you two return."

In the back of my mind, I knew he'd check in and let either José or Bevin know everything, but I didn't care. I just wanted wings and wind.

Once past the pool, I slowly stripped down. I would not deny or confirm rumors that I needed assistance with the shirt, or that I lost my balance and would've fallen without the help of Alex's quick hands.

Sitting on the ground, I hugged my knees and focused on Swan. My belly tickled, like feathers waving about, and then a lightness I craved enveloped me. The shift to Swan always lightened my body, but with the addition of the pregnancy, the cessation of gravity on me was bliss like no other. We worried about the frequency of my shifts, so I wanted to enjoy my flight knowing it may be my last before the babies were born.

I honked my joy before spreading my wings, hopping, and using all my energy to take to the air. It had taken two years of training and exercises with Owen to learn how to launch from the ground, but now I could do it. I wouldn't ever tell him, but I really appreciated what he did.

The clear blue sky, barely spotted with white clouds, beckoned me. I let the cool airwaves dictate my direction as I circled high above the property. Joy filled me as I stretched my wings and flew.

My path was lazy. No highway speeds for me, though it was quite possible in this form. I just wanted some time to relax with a streamlined body.

As I surveyed the land, a movement on the ground caught my attention. Dipping lower, I saw a wolf on the edge of the property. The way it moved, awkward and unnatural, it couldn't be all animal. With a sigh, I ate up a bit more of my lowering reserve of energy and tapped into my epsilon ability to mentally contact Alex.

"Hey, Jade, looking good up there. What's up?"

There's a werewolf slinking onto our lands. I'm going to contact José next, just wanted to give you a heads-up as well, in case they come closer.

"Sounds good. He should be out of his meeting."

Of course everyone knew José's schedule. I wanted to scream. Instead, I let out a honk of annoyance.

Dropping my connection with Alex, I send out a mental tug to my alpha.

"Chica, is this important?"

Really? Do you think I'm contacting you for ice cream and pickles?

His sigh came down the line, loud and clear.

"Sorry, work's hectic. What's up?"

I took a calming breath. *No, I'm sorry. I'm in a short mood. I'm flying—*

"You're what?"

No! Do not get sidetracked. I needed to move, and Swan is easy and comfortable.

"And seriously dangerous if you fall from the sky, chica."

José, focus. There's a wolf on our property. I'm going to land, go in the house, and let you or Alex, or whomever, deal with it, okay? I just figured you'd like to know.

Silence preceded his snarl. I watched the ground as I slowly made my way back to the house, focusing on any other possible wolves invading. *"Thank you. Thank you for not asking to be part of this. I'll be home soon to figure this out. Tell Alex that they shouldn't deal with it either."*

Sounds good. I'm going to land, shift, and eat. See you soon.

A blast of his contentment at my contacting him mixed with his irritation at the situation came down the line as I almost made it back home.

I'd been so focused on the conversation and looking for pests in our woods, I didn't notice the gaggle of geese until I was upon them. They started to honk and dart toward me. I swooped, banking hard to avoid the beasts as the mean bullies attacked. Dipping lower than they were willing to fly, I made to where Alex waited for me and shifted.

The weight of what felt like cement filling my bones, and the babies filling my belly, nearly toppled me over, and I howled. I already missed my swan form. *Can I just stay a bird until the babies come?*

Alex ran up and helped me with my shirt. They tugged my hands and I stood, almost pitching over. Leaning hard on the smaller packmate, I finagled the rest of my clothes. The world spun as I tried to stand tall. Too much energy used and not enough food.

Alex lowered me back down to the grass. "I'll get you a shake, or something, then I'll check out the wolf."

"No, just the shake. José is on his way back. We'll wait for him here."

The side of their mouth twitched. "Oh, good. Then I can show him the video I got of you and the geese."

Chapter 3 - Stranger In A Strange Land
Bevin

"Dr. Cortez-Green. I don't want to die." Large brown eyes gazed up at me, ready to drop tears.

My heart hurt for this nine-year-old with cancer. "I know. And if I have my way, you won't. We're putting together a treatment plan for you, you know that. The first step is to believe in your future and fight for it. You are sick, but that doesn't mean you can't also live."

Her lip trembled as she nodded. "Okay. I'll try. I'm sorry."

I sighed. "Don't apologize. I just want you to be strong and fight."

On her other side, her mother squeezed her hand. "See, dear, I told you it wasn't over. Dr. Cortez-Green believes in you. We all do. You just need to believe in yourself."

It warmed my heart to hear such support from family.

"Okay. I think we're done for now. I'll send a nurse in to talk to you about what happens next. I've put in a referral for you to see a specialist and get a second opinion. If the referral doesn't go through, you should talk to your primary pediatrician. Until then, I've sent a prescription for pain meds to your pharmacy on file.

You're finally free to go home ... once the nurse finishes all the paperwork."

The mom gave a small smile. "Who knew when we came to the emergency department thinking she was sick it would lead to all this? So many days in the hospital. Thank you again for being so kind."

"Of course. Good luck."

I headed to my office. I had a few minutes free, and I needed to decompress after that. There was also a mug of coffee and a piece of chocolate cake from someone's birthday calling my name. If Jade knew she'd missed the cake, she'd be pissed. I could bring a piece home to her ... nah! I smiled to myself. Oscar spoiled her with chocolate shakes.

With a groan, I sat. I wasn't old enough to be this sore, but my shifts were long. My pocket vibrated and I pulled out my phone to see a call from José. Just seeing his name made my insides heat. It still amazed me that he was my husband and we'd been married for over eight years. Hell, we were about to have kids together.

"Hey, aren't you at work?" A call during the day was never a good sign.

He sighed. "Jade contacted me. A foreign wolf is on our lands."

"She ... contacted you, like via phone?" I could only hope.

"Like from the air, flying. Alone." The snarl reverberated through the phone. I couldn't blame him; anger threatened to burn through my voice as well.

"She went flying?" I stood. My eyebrows wouldn't get high enough if I didn't.

"We can talk to her about that later. She said she was too tired to even think about approaching the stranger on the property."

That got my attention. "I'm on my way. It'll take me a few minutes to clear my cases for the day, but don't do anything without me."

"Love you." The words grounded me like nothing else could.

"Love you, too."

Wavering between frustration that Jade had flown and appreciation that she'd called José about the stranger, I decided to bring her some cake. It would give her something to focus on while we went out and investigated. Finding doctors to cover my patients wasn't easy, but everyone loved Jade and when I told them she wasn't feeling well, they all but kicked me out.

When I got home, I found her draped in the backyard, half in the grass, half on the pool deck. Her clothes were askew, and I assumed Alex had helped her put them on. When she saw me, she started to struggle to get up on her own.

"Want help?"

She glared at me.

Alex smiled. "Want to see my footage while Jade does it all herself?"

I shook my head at the ridiculousness of the situation but watched the swan versus geese video. *This is gold!*

After Jade got to her butt, I tilted my head at her. "Do you want to be out here, in a chair, or inside and more comfortable?"

Her eyes narrowed at me. "I'm not an invalid, you know. I can walk on my own."

"Yes, dear. I know you can. You've been able to walk since you were a babe, but you're sitting here, not walking."

"I happen to think it's a lovely day."

She happened to look like a beached whale and miserable. "Okay, I guess I'll have to let José eat the piece of chocolate birthday cake, then."

"There was cake? Don't you dare!" She started to push herself up and huffed in annoyance. I slipped behind her and lifted her to her feet. She grumbled, but I kept an arm around her waist, letting her lean on me. Despite her protests, she accepted my help, which I was grateful for. I knew she had to be exhausted to be willing to admit defeat, even this subtly, so quickly.

Inside Were House, she sat in the living room in one of the recliner chairs, her chosen nest for the last few weeks. I gave her the cake, Alex brought her milk, and Oscar, our chef extraordinaire, brought her a chocolate shake. *I have no idea how she eats so many sweets! Now, if we're lucky, she'd fall asleep before José and I get back from our investigation.*

In the backyard, I found José searching the edge of the woods. I wrapped my arms around him in a hug and leaned down for a kiss. This was my home. It didn't matter where we were, if I had him, I would be fine.

"How was your day?"

"Rough, but we can discuss that later. Let's deal with this." I shook a set of clothes I held for the stranger to indicate our goal.

We wanted to talk to him, and Jade hadn't mentioned seeing a base camp or clothing. It was easier to bring something for them to wear than to deal with a naked human. "Do you want to take point?"

His face scrunched up as he gazed out into the trees as if he could see the person. His eyes shot up at the honking sound of geese. "I wonder if Jade ran into those mean beasties on her outing."

I snorted. "Alex has a video. You should ask them to show you when we get home."

He bit his bottom lip. "Jade and Geese, the saga continues." After another few seconds of thinking, José nodded. "Okay, I'll take point. You be the fierce enforcer wolf. Your beautiful black beast is scarier than my red wolf."

After handing him the spare clothes, I stripped and handed him my clothes. I then got down to my hands and knees. Calling to my wolf, it exploded around me. It felt like the person I was, the human, got wrapped up and hidden away, while the beast ripped its way out. Others talked about bones and hair receding and regrowing, but to me, it was humanity being tucked away in lieu of the black monster.

Once the wolf was free, I stretched, sniffing the air and ground. Scents came to me, powerful and plentiful. The dry dirt, the minty eucalyptus, amongst other trees and foliage, the deadly geese, and the trails of all our pack. I loved how much more I could parse out in this form. José placed his hand on my head, and I heard, *"Go."*

One of the biggest secrets kept amongst the alphas was that we had limited speech between us. The ability was more so with mates. Jade could speak to anyone she wanted to; she was a marvel. No one understood her abilities, those of the epsilon wolf. Her magic was beyond reason. She probably did more than she technically should've been able to, but no one gave her limits.

The secret only alphas knew, and somehow hadn't gotten out was, between two strong and connected alphas, or mates, we could say single words, or send images and impressions. The latter was easier because it was more in line with how actual wolves communicated.

José and I headed out in the direction Jade had given my mate, José jogging next to me. It was easier for me to navigate the physical obstacles—trees and shrubs—while José could ignore the scents. For some reason this interloper hadn't chosen a spot along one of our usual trails.

I enjoyed it when we were both wolves better, but any time we could run together strengthened our bond and warmed my soul.

It didn't take us long to find the brown wolf in the woods. He slunk towards some bushes as if trying to hide. José snorted. "Not only can I see you, we can smell you. You are on our property. Since this isn't a normal running ground for wolves and you aren't acting like a regular wolf, I know you understand me. Come out and shift. I have a t-shirt and shorts."

A small whine came from the bush. I released a bit of my alpha power to encourage him to move.

Another whimper, and he finally emerged. He was small for a werewolf, and he hung his head low. I just gazed at him, head tilted, watching him.

José sighed. "Please shift."

His eyes momentarily cut to José before landing solidly back on me. He knew where the real threat lay. José had power, but I emoted danger.

A loving hand curled into the fur on my head, and I wanted to purr—not that werewolves purred. In my head, José's voice whispered, *"Less."*

A low growl rumbled from my gut, but I pulled up my mantle a bit, blocking some of the power that was part of being alpha.

Gratitude radiated from José as the wolf stood a bit taller.

"Now, shift, or we'll have to push the issue."

Even though this small creature wasn't one of our wolves, if we wanted to, we could force him to shift. Either one of us had the ability to do it. It would be better if the wolf chose to shift on his own.

The brown wolf snarled and stood his ground. In his eyes, he held the defiance of an animal ready to fight for his place in the world. Ironically, his rank didn't feel that high.

We waited for another few beats, but it was apparent he wouldn't shift. *What the hell is he here for if not to talk to us?*

In a fit of frustration, I released a blast of power with a command. *Shift!*

The wolf howled in fear, the sweet, sugary scent blanketing the area. His body began to contort.

José knelt next to me. "Shift, too. I have your clothes."

Becoming human was like unwrapping a gift. As painful as the shift felt, the joy at knowing I'd be myself, male, and mate to José at the end superseded anything else.

Before my first shift, I was assigned female. It never fit me. My wolf had always been male, and in a miracle that still brought me joy, when I first shifted from wolf to human, my soul, spirit, and wolf, brought me back the way I always knew my body should be. It took a little more than that, but in the end, I had male bits. I would never understand anyone not loving being a werewolf.

I transformed faster than the brown wolf. He was still shifting as I slipped on my slacks and button-down white shirt. I'd debated putting on something casual but decided time was more important than what I wore.

When the stranger was human, his shift that of a new wolf—slow, awkward, and painful looking—José tossed the clothes near his hand. He hurriedly slipped on the plain black T-shirt and gray shorts. He stood but kept his eyes down. He felt submissive, but he acted like a very new wolf, he could be zeta ... too new to tell.

I shook my head. He was just a kid. "Who are you, and why are you here?"

His eyes met mine without his head moving. He froze, then dropped his focus back down to the ground. "I ... ah ... maybe I should just go."

José growled low. He was getting annoyed, and very little annoyed my husband. "Who are you?" He spoke slowly, enunciating each word. "Why are you here?"

"Garrett Turner, sir. I ... well, I'm a werewolf."

I slumped. This would take all night. "Yes, we know. You just shifted in front of us. Can we fast-forward this story a bit, please?"

"Lily said you could help me."

That gave me pause. I reached out for José's hand. He linked his fingers with mine. Images of people flashed between us. When we first mated, this would give me a headache, the speed of visual communication, the complexity of it all. Now I could keep up a conversation while throwing snapshots back and forth to José.

"Were you bitten?" I was trying to get something from him, but he didn't seem to want to just talk.

"Oh, like her dad, Tyler? No."

Got it! I sent an image of a man and his daughter from the Wisconsin pack to José. He sent one back of the same pair, and I had to work to keep a blank face. Tyler's family had been attacked. His wife had died, he'd been changed, and luckily Lily hadn't been bitten. River, Jade's dad, and one of the Wisconsin alphas, invited him to join their pack, gave him a job, and gave him hope for his future.

José stepped towards him, letting our physical connection drop. "Then how is it you're a werewolf? How did you end up in our woods?"

Garrett gulped, and I could see him fighting to not step back. "I don't know. When I was a baby I was adopted. My parents ... they died, but a family took me in. Anyway, I was brought up as a normal kid, you know ... normal. I decided to go to college at UC - Santa Cruz. I met Lily there. Last month during the full moon—oh, my God!" He grabbed his stomach and looked like he would be sick. "I turned into a wolf! But she was there, and she helped. If she hadn't, I have no idea what I'd've done. There's a whole arboretum by the school, but it's still not safe."

José lowered his voice. "Did you bite Lily or anyone else?"

"No!" Garrett's hands flew up, and he shook his head vehemently. "I swear, I promise, I didn't."

I could smell the truth of his words. "It's okay, you may not know this, but you should ... or will. As a werewolf, you can smell lies."

"I'm not lying."

"I know." Part of me wished for Jade's ability to calm. "That's what I'm saying. I ... we," I waved my hand between me and José, "can hear the truth of your words."

He started to tremble. "So, you believe me?"

Part of me wanted to roll my eyes and walk away. This kid was too much. A new wolf at this age when we were about to have babies ... but we couldn't leave him on his own, not this ignorant. Beyond the security risk of an untrained lone wolf, he was here for a reason.

I licked my lips. "So, you've told us who you are, now tell us why you came."

He let his eyes drift up to mine once again, but then dropped just as fast. I wasn't sure what was up with that. If he stayed, he'd need to talk with Brooke. "I want you to help me, make it go away. I want to be normal again ... you know, to not be a werewolf."

Chapter 4 - Pulling Rank
Bevin

Jade was exactly where we'd left her. She looked content in her chair with Enoch on her lap. The cat was a cute fuzzball of love. He leapt away when he saw us enter with a stranger. Jade's eyes narrowed and then her eyebrow rose. "You brought the stray back? Into our den?" Her face tightened, then she shut her eyes, took a breath, and stood, a bit wobbly.

I darted over to help her make it to the back door, though if looks could kill, *I* may not have made it. Even with my help, it took some time, but we arrived as José answered her.

"Chica, relax. We wouldn't endanger our future goose-wrangler, now would we?" His eyes twinkled at the reminder of her earlier escapades.

Holding out a hand to the newcomer, she gave what *could have* been a friendly smile, but wasn't. "Welcome to our home. I'm Jade."

Garrett gazed at her for a moment, smelling minty from his confusion. There were too many firsts for him. Then he took her hand. "Hi, um, I'm Garrett. Nice to meet you."

She stepped away and sat at the dining room table. Oscar slipped a mug of chamomile tea in front of her, and she took a sip, apparently without even noticing. Then she glared at José. "I can't believe Alex has digital proof this time of me and the freaking geese. I can only imagine what she and Violet are going to do with that. Just when I thought I'd finally lived that incident down."

She hadn't lived it down. If we all lived to be a thousand years old, she'd never live it down. It was cute she thought that, though.

José led Garrett to a chair, and I headed to sit next to Jade, rubbing her back to alleviate some of her stress. "Want food? We can eat, talk, and figure things out." Food was a great distraction for any werewolf ... or werepanther.

Before she could answer, Enoch yowled from somewhere in the den, letting us know *his* thoughts on the matter. Then the cat sauntered in from the hall where he'd disappeared, leapt up to an empty couch with a blanket, kneaded it a couple of times, and laid down with a loud purr. From nowhere, Red joined him. We watched, until they were settled. The white cat's purr made his opinion on the situation clear.

When the cats' antics were done, a chocolate shake appeared at Jade's spot. Oscar could make those things magically in the kitchen. I swore I never even heard the blender working as he made them. When I was in his domain, there was never a mess from the blending of the shake. I leaned towards Jade's ear and whispered, "He's magic."

She giggled, finally relaxing.

Garrett took the seat across from Jade, José next to him. Before any food was brought out, Brooke sashayed out and gave Jade a kiss on the cheek, then sat on her other side.

They were the most unlikely couple I could imagine. After years of being enemies in high school, their antagonistic relationship morphed into major clashing once Brooke joined the pack. I had no idea how they landed here. I loved that Jade was happy and finally found someone to be with, but if someone had offered me a million dollars ten years ago on a bet that those two would ever end up together, I'd've laughed in their face ... and lost a lot of money.

The scents of food floated out from the kitchen, and Jade moaned. "I feel like I haven't eaten in days. These pups are going to be my death."

I squeezed my face tight. Someone was going to mess this up, and I was going to have to kill them. There was no other option at that point. "Jade! Gods above, no information."

"Bev, for crying out loud. I would call any kid a pup, be it from a werefamily or normal family. Sarah and I would call kids at day care facility 'pups' when we'd walk past them before she even knew about wereanimals. Chill." She must be hungry, judging by the snap of her response.

I narrowed my eyes at her, not sure I believed that story. Before I could say more, platters with sizzling steak, chicken, and shrimp appeared from the kitchen. Oscar placed other platters with grilled onions and peppers on the table in between the others. Perfectly warmed-up tortillas were next, followed by a tray with cheese, sour cream, salsa, pico de gallo, hot sauce, and a bowl of chips. My mouth watered and I was totally distracted.

Both Brooke and I set about creating fajitas for Jade before we started on our own food. It was somewhat of a game, or challenge. With two wereanimals, a shifter bird, and however many babies in her belly, Jade could probably sit and eat all day. She got tired and would stop, eventually. If we could keep her plate full, she wouldn't always notice how much she'd eaten, so everyone contributed.

After I made Jade's wrap, I created the perfect steak and shrimp fajita for myself. Spices exploded in my mouth, and I sank back and enjoyed it. Halfway through, I looked down and saw a second fajita on my plate, I slid it over to Jade's plate and continued to eat.

As the group took the edge off their hunger, the room stayed silent. Once everyone had satiated the sharpest of their need, José leaned back. "So, Garrett, start at the beginning."

Garrett slowly lowered his fajita. "I don't really know what to tell you." He placed his food on his plate. "I was at school and felt weird. Lily knew what was happening to me. I didn't know why." He looked around the table at all the faces, and I noticed his hands begin to tremble. "She forced me to head out to the woods. I wanted to go to the hospital. She told me to get naked. I was freaking out and didn't know what she was about. My mind stuttered and then my body cramped. Next thing I knew, my body, my hair, my bones, there were ... God, it was awful." His face drained of all color. "She had climbed a tree. I attacked my bag, destroying it after my ... um, shift? That's what Lily told me to call it. Once my tail was between my legs, she climbed down, helped me with my clothes, and told me to run for a bit and come back."

José's voice, calm yet commanding, filled the space when Garrett faltered. "Did you hunt when you ran? Find a river and drink? Or just run?"

Scent sweet with nerves, Garrett shifted his gaze to my mate. "I ... the instinct you know. I found a rodent. I couldn't help myself."

"No reason to apologize, we all understand here. We're all hunters. We're safe."

Despite the words, his fear amped up.

Next to me, Jade grunted. There was a moment where she took some audible breaths, then I felt the wave. She'd learned to aim her epsilon calm. Despite that, its effects were still like a blanket, and a bit of the stress of the day left me. Across from us, Garrett slumped.

His eyes grew wide. "Did you drug the food?"

José rubbed his forehead. "No, we just took away a bit of your stress, werewolf style. Now, you hunted, then returned to Lily?"

"Oh, um, yeah. She told me to shift back. My clothes were a bit worse for wear, but I managed. Then she explained a lot of stuff to me." He dropped one of his hands to his lap and took a shaking sip of water. After a few moments, he continued. "After, like the next day, she told me to come here. It was a couple of weeks ago. I know we're close to another full moon. I just ... how can you all stand it?"

He looked close to tears.

Jade huffed and seemed to want to get things wrapped up. "You're a werewolf and you don't remember being bitten. Moreover, you don't want to be one."

He nodded.

"I hate to tell you this, but it isn't something you can turn on and turn off. What Lily offered you wasn't salvation from a curse, it was a place to learn. We aren't a group who doesn't like what we are, we are a happy pack. We can teach you. We can help you find a pack that suits you. But we are not, in any way, shape, or form, unhappy. Nor will we tell you how to not be what you were born to be."

I wanted to pound my fist in the air and cheer. A part of me wanted to smirk and lift an eyebrow in challenge. Maybe let out a bit of my power and show him who was boss. I didn't do any of those things. I sat as passively as I could. I'd done this before, let Jade explain things, and sat back—the silent power behind the voice of our pack.

Sometimes, José did the talking. There were times it was me. Of the three of us, I was the most intimidating. That was another thing high school me would've never believed. Back then, I was a class-act nerd, not at all intimidating. Now I was both.

Garrett nodded. "Okay, I'm sorry. I'm really confused, and scared, and ... everything smells. And I feel and hear and ... I don't know what's going on."

Alex chuckled softly. "We can help you with all of that. We've all been through the change. Dealing with all the extra senses just takes training. Especially when it comes with learning about this freaky new world."

He snapped his head to them. "Really? You weren't born with all," he waved his hand over his body, "this? You haven't always been part of a ... er ... pack?"

"Me?" Alex asked, covering their mouth as they laughed. "No. I was attacked when I was in college. Almost died. Like you, I knew nothing about werewolves or," they hesitated, "well, anything really. It takes time. But I'm happier now than before. The pack is family."

Garrett leaned back in his chair, picking up his food. "Yeah, okay. So, what happens now?"

Jade sipped her chocolate shake. *Is that her first, second, or third?* "Well, we'll set you up in a guest room and when my brother gets home, he'll figure out a training program for you. Trust me, he lives for this type of thing. You'll learn all about being a werewolf. As for me, I've been thinking, with Christmas so close—" she shifted her focus to José, "—and my feeling fantastic, I may be able to do a bit of work for a few more days. Nothing too strenuous, have you just—"

"No." I'd heard enough. We'd had this conversation, and she was out for the next three months if I had to tie her down.

"I'm fine. And I'm bored. I can't shift, according to you, or fly, or work, or have coffee, or go in the hot tub. Gah! What's left?"

Before I could tell her what was left, Brooke wrapped an arm around her waist. "Well, maybe we could rent a small house by the beach in Santa Cruz. It's close. We could sun. You could do your best beached whale impression. It would be like a pre-honeymoon."

Jade froze, her mouth dropping open.

I realized my mouth hung open as well. *Did I miss the gossip around here? Since when are they going on a honeymoon?*

Brooke pushed Jade's chair so she faced her. Then Brooke dropped to one knee, pulling a ring from somewhere. "Jade Stone. We've had quite the ride, you and me. I was wondering if you'd do me the honor of becoming my wife."

Chapter 5 - Full House
Jade

On my left hand, I had a silver ring with a braided band that Brooke had given me for our engagement. It had sapphire stones that formed a heart. In the center were three small diamonds. My heart skipped a beat every time I looked at it. *I'm getting married. I'm marrying Brooke. I love Brooke. The girl who used to torment me is now my safe space.*

My mind whirled.

I sat by the pool with a cup of hot cocoa and a croque madame sandwich. The new ring on my finger caught the light from the sun, sparkling. On my right hand, I wore the ring Bevin and José had given me years ago with images of my animals and my mental landscape. It was a small symbol of our pack and brought me peace whenever I started to stress or spiral. For some reason, despite the holidays, or because of them, I'd been feeling very stressed.

Once done with my food, I pushed myself up and started walking—waddling—around the pool. What I wanted more than anything was to walk into town. I craved ice cream. I imagined I could taste toasted s'mores delight. I sighed at the ridiculous thought.

By the time I made it back to the house, I found José standing there, as if he was waiting for me.

I narrowed my eyes at him. "Don't you have work today?"

"Chica, it's three days until Christmas. I've taken the next week and a half off." He waved his elbow in offering. "Your dad's company may work a person hard, but it isn't that bad."

"You're going to walk around the pool with me?"

He tilted his head. "Do you have a better idea?"

I let my shoulders slump. I had a lot of better ideas. The question was, could I *do* any of them? If I tried, I'd probably end up on my butt and I'd never get up. "What I'd really like is to walk to town and get an ice cream cone."

He smiled wide. "Do you think you can make it that far? Walking is good for you, or so I'm told."

My hands flew to my sides in an overly comical shrug. "I have no idea. This inability to do anything is driving me crazy. Your kids aren't even born and they're already driving me nuts."

"They're your kiddos too, chica. You know that, right?"

"Whatever." Despite my snapping at him, a warmth infused me. I was so excited to be a mom. Every time the pups moved, even when they kicked, I imagined them terrorizing the whole pack. I knew these rugrats would rule the roost.

He chuckled, a knowing smile on his face. "How about we walk into town together? We'll get ice cream. Then we can walk back. If that ends up being too much for you, then we'll call for a ride."

My mouth twitched in a small smile. "I'm being a bit dramatic, I know, but thank you."

As we walked through the house 'O Christmas Tree' played from the living room. José immediately started singing, and I elbowed him in his side. He chuckled. "What? I love singing. I'll serenade you all the way to the ice cream shop."

"Not if you want to live to see Christmas ... or your kids." I was mostly kidding, though the music was driving me batty.

From the living room, amongst the swan and wolf Christmas lights Owen had especially made for the season and the huge tree that dominated the space, Alex called out. They sat by the tree, surrounded by gifts and their husband Quinn. "Ice cream? I'm so in!"

They leapt up. Quinn, holding a book, snorted. "Not me. I need some peace and quiet before we visit your family." The two of them were heading back to Alex's family's farm for Christmas tomorrow. Alex didn't see their family much, but their visits seemed to go better with Quinn along. Though their family had never been the most supportive, they loved Quinn.

The walk into town was fantastic. I got to stretch my legs, the weather was ideal, lovely people to talk with, the only problem was, it was too slow ... amazingly slow. José was treating me like I was made of porcelain. *I can walk faster than this!* It felt like a year had gone by and we were only halfway there.

"And then this woman came in to have her pet checked out. A day as a vet, you know how my life goes! Anyway, you wouldn't believe her outfit; probably cost more than my car. She had one of those dogs that people carry in their purses, you know the ones: small, yappy, annoying dogs." Alex smiled at me and then at José.

They loved dogs and probably didn't think any of them were actually annoying.

I narrowed my eyes at them. "Was the dog at least cute?"

They snorted. "So cute. She came in because all her friends had dogs that were more willing to stay in their purses, but hers always tried to escape. She wanted a drug to keep the dog sedated."

A low growl of disapproval came from José. It could've been the drugs, but it may have been the idea of walking around with an animal in a purse. Both things seemed pretty awful.

"Anyway," Alex continued, ignoring our irate alpha. "This woman plops her purse on the table and the animal hisses."

My eyebrow flew up. "You mean snarls, right?"

"Oh, no, I mean hisses. The nincompoop of a rich woman had found a cat, a big cat—an exotic one I'll grant you—but definitely not a dog. Here look at this picture."

I held my stomach, from laughing so hard. The picture was a cat, very clearly a cat, but I'd never seen a cat that looked so much like a dog. Someone who didn't care for animals could possibly be confused.

José stopped walking to laugh. "Oh, my gods. I need that picture. That's going on Owen's birthday cake next month with the words: *Have a dog cat of a good year!*"

I snorted and Alex beamed. They said, "That's excellent. You can run the order to the bakery while Jade and I enjoy our ice cream. Then Brooke can come and pick us up."

The idea that I couldn't walk home hurt, but Alex was right. It'd be midnight before I made it on foot.

There were two recliner chairs in the living room. I'd adopted one as my very own during the pregnancy. I had blankets, pillows, and a small table for my books and treats. Everyone in the pack knew to avoid sitting in that seat.

When we got home, I felt tired, sore, and defeated that I couldn't walk back. I stood at the door and gaped. Garrett sat in my cocoon. He sat under my blanket, read from my favorite book, and had Enoch, the traitorous cat, on his lap, as if he had the right to the spot and all my goodies.

José sighed.

Brooke stomped over, shaking her head. "I know you're not from the pack, but what about a chair with blankets, a pillow, and pregnancy books, tells you to use it? There are hundreds of other seats, why take this one?"

Garrett's mouth dropped open, then he snapped it shut. "I ... uh. It looked comfy."

Her mouth tightened. "You know what? I think we need to go out to the pool and talk. I hear you're struggling with the transition to being a wolf. I can help."

"You can take it away?"

A bark of laughter erupted from Brooke. A sound so foreign, I gaped at her. She shook her head. "No, no one can do that, which we explained to you last night. Let's go talk."

She led him out, and I switched out my blankets to ones that didn't smell like him before I sank into my nest. Enoch tried to join me, but I shooed him away. I was annoyed at his betrayal. I cuddled with Annabelle and let my feet rest.

I didn't want to move again ... ever. I'd live off the scents Oscar created from the kitchen: pastry, sauce, sage, and chicken? Oh, dinner would be good tonight. *I may have to move again after all.*

Just as I picked up my eBook reader, Milo came out from one of the hallways. "There's a car at the gate."

I groaned, glaring towards the gate. I held contempt for whomever dared to enter our territory. They were lucky I couldn't cast curses.

José pulled out his phone before I could. His smile lit up as he typed on his phone and walked to the door.

The bounce in his step made my feet throb. *How dare he be peppy!* "Should I stand up? You know it takes me a while."

"Up to you." His eyes twinkled.

"Who's here?" I started to push myself up. I wasn't sure when going from sitting to standing had become such a process. I'd finally gotten my butt to the edge of the seat when a whirlwind of high-energy teen flew into the house, past José, and wrapped itself around me.

"Pebble!" I pronounced. "What are you doing here?"

She giggled. "Hi, Jade." She pulled back. "I'm so excited to see you." Her sparkling eyes, practically the same color as my jewel-green ones, almost glowed as they looked around the room. "Tree. Gifts. Lights. Where's the festive music? I mean, there isn't snow, you need to do something to bring the Christmas cheer."

I squeezed my sister. "Yes, Merry Christmas. No music, it was driving me crazy. José can't stop singing. Now, why are you here? Why aren't you in Wisconsin? And did you come alone?"

A woman walked into the house, dropped her bags, and gave José a big hug. I smiled. "Aunt Allison!"

Pebble stood by my chair. "I was sitting in the living room the other day and I had one of my premonitions. It was more of a feeling than the normal images this time, thank the gods. Anyway, I knew that me and Aunt Allison had to be here ... like, right away, before Christmas. So, here we are."

I finally got myself up and waddled over to Aunt Allison and José, my feet screaming, but I ignored them. Aunt Allison's face softened as she tried to hug me over my enlarged belly. "My goodness, Jade, you're the size of a tiny house. I guess that makes sense because you're currently the house for some wild and crazy kiddos, aren't you?"

"Gah! I just want these kiddos, as you call them, out of me, Aunt Allison. I want to be able to move again ... and sneeze ... without making a mess."

Aunt Allison chuckled. "I know, but once they're out of you, then you'll wish for sleep. It's all about sacrifice from here on out. What are you willing to give up for these new creatures you've created that you'll love with all your heart?"

I paused and gazed at my aunt. I knew she didn't expect an answer, at least not right away. "I'll tell you my answer in the next three to twenty-three years, give or take a lifetime." I tottered back and forth until I was a few feet from Aunt Allison. "So, what was the hurry? Why did you two need to be here today?"

Allison shrugged. "I'm not sure. But since I was told it was imperative, I didn't fight it. I also don't have any kids at home, so I was okay with missing the family Christmas. And because I brought Pebble, your parents are holding off on the gift exchange until we get back."

Oscar emerged from the kitchen. "Well, it's nice that y'all came to visit, but let's eat the chicken pot pies before they get cold."

Pebble sat next to me. The food, as always, was amazing. I turned to her. "So, are you staying through Christmas?"

She shrugged. "I guess. I just knew we needed to be here. You know the details I get."

José's eyes danced and he smiled at Pebble. "Christmas *and* New Year's? That's wonderful!"

I whipped my head towards Pebble and my mind put puzzle pieces together. "Did you really have a premonition or did Bev call you to come as a distraction because I kept fighting to go back to work?"

Pebble bumped her shoulder into me. "You know that isn't the case. Anyway, it's my winter break at school. I need to get back after two weeks. And Mom and Dad are coming, too."

The fork stopped halfway to my mouth. "What now?"

"What? You thought they'd spend Christmas without either of us? Nah. Mom's done with her semester, but they held off on coming because Dad needed to finish a job."

Aunt Allison nodded. "Maybe your premonition knew I'd be the one with the time."

José shook his head, looking off into the distance. "Maybe it will be a medical issue."

Eyes widening, I shook my head. I didn't even want the words out in the wild.

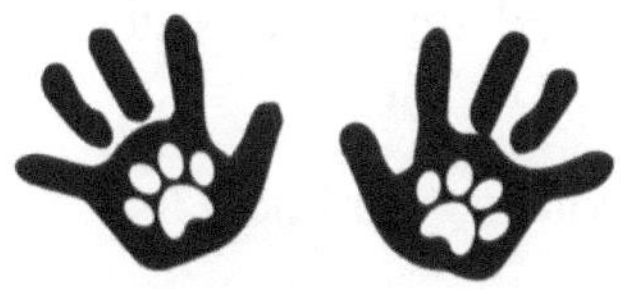

Chapter 6 - Two's Company...
Jade

My room was the second in the hallway. I'd always been an early riser, but after I was bitten by a werepanther, it seemed like early mornings were completely my time. Brooke sometimes woke up with me, and then threatened to kick me out of bed if I messed with her beauty sleep. Being pregnant, I didn't *think* she'd kick me out, but with Brooke, one never knew.

With my huge belly, I felt as wide as I was tall, and getting from the bed to the bathroom, the bathroom to the closet, and the closet to the dining room, seemed to take half my morning. By the time I got there, it felt like most of the house was up. I lowered myself into a chair, and as always, Oscar had a large mug of tea and a plate of peanut butter toast and eggs ready for me. He also gave me a plate with fruit.

The theory was that I was building bodies—wereanimal bodies—and I should eat a lot of protein. Although I needed little encouragement on that front, everyone found ways to add more protein into my diet.

I missed coffee. I tried not to complain, but I don't think I was very successful. I was almost done with my first breakfast when

Pebble appeared. I gazed up at my sister. "What are you doing here?"

"It's later in Wisconsin, you know that."

"I do, but you're a teen. You're supposed to sleep in until noon or later, right?"

"I was hoping we could take a walk—"

My face scrunched up. It wasn't that I didn't want to walk—I walked every day—but she was used to the normal me.

"Like in the back yard. Can we walk to the park gate and back? I know you aren't up to your normal distance."

I smiled up at her. "Yeah, sure. I'm game."

While we spoke, Oscar brought out more food. Another plate for me, and one for Pebble.

Throughout the years, everyone in the pack had tried to get Oscar to sit and relax. He did join us at times, but he loved to play in the kitchen. He once told me that he woke early—and he did. No matter how early I rose, he was always in the kitchen when I came out for coffee ... or tea. But his theory was, as long as he was up, why not do what he enjoyed?

Once we finished eating, I heaved myself to my feet, and we headed out. Aunt Alison slipped from the kitchen. She smiled. "Talk to you later, Oscar."

My mouth dropped as I marveled at her audacity. Oscar usually guarded his den worse than a dragon. "He allowed you in his domain?"

She patted my shoulder as she joined Pebble and me. "We've been friends for years, dear, and I've never been a disaster in the kitchen." The citrus scent of her amusement wafted to me.

"I'm not that bad," I groused.

She laughed as Pebble shut the back door behind us.

Once we'd passed the pool, my pace slowed. "Sorry, I walk so slow." We walked along the tree line in the shade. It may have been December, but the sun was hot and there wasn't a breeze today.

Aunt Allison chuckled. "Jade, dear, you're carrying three pups. What did you expect? To run a marathon?"

I eyed Pebble. "You told her?"

"Of course I did. She's your doula."

I sighed. "You two live three thousand miles away. The chances you're going to be in California when these three pop out isn't very likely."

Pebble put her hand on my arm. "You can never know the future. You just have to relax and let things happen the way they're supposed to happen."

"Are you being you, or your wolf?"

She slumped. "I don't even know anymore. So ... do the boys know you're having three?"

We walked for a few more steps. "José knows there are three; he doesn't know much more. Bevin knows there are multiples, but he gets upset if I give him any more details. Just so you know. He doesn't want to know anything."

"What about names? You have three babies growing in there. They all need names." The concern rolled off her in a soothing sandalwood scent.

I smiled. "We have a list of possible names. I had the boys each come up with their top four names for boys and girls. They decided I could pick the final name for each. We determined this idea early on when we had no way of knowing how many pups I carried. When the question arose concerning what happens if not enough names were on the small lists, I started delineating ways I could kill them. They got the idea."

Both Pebble and Aunt Allison laughed.

"So, I know we're not out here to discuss these soon-to-be rugrats. Tell me, Pebble, what's on your mind?"

Color drained from her face, and she bit her lower lip. "Well, you know that I've always wanted to join your pack. I asked when you guys were first forming, but you told me to wait. Finish school."

"Yep, I remember." And I did. It had broken my heart to tell her 'no' that day.

"Well, here's the thing. You left, Owen left, hell, even José left. It's like all the teens have up and gone away."

It wasn't true. She was exaggerating. There were still several pack teens in Wisconsin. Even Tanner's son was still around, and Tanner had power. I couldn't remember if his son was alpha level, but it wouldn't surprise me if he was, considering Tanner's strength.

I narrowed my eyes at her. "What are you trying to tell me, sis?"

Her voice lowered and Aunt Allison slid her hand around her waist. *In my condition I'd probably land us both on our butts.* "I applied to a lot of colleges, including the ones in Wisconsin. You know that, right?"

This was taking too long. She had to get to the point. "Okay, so what you're hinting at is, you don't want to leave the cold Midwest for the beauty of California."

Her eyes grew to the size of saucers. "It isn't that I don't love you and want to be part of this pack. You know that, right?"

"I do, sweetheart. You have power; you always have. And you want to stay in Wisconsin."

"I do. I was accepted into UW-Madison, and Mom and Dad want me to take over. They're going to start training me this summer after I graduate high school."

A sadness washed through me. Not for the loss of my sister from my pack, but for the loss of her childhood. Not only were our parents asking her to become the leader of a large and powerful pack, they were asking her to do it alone. She didn't have a mate, someone to run the pack with her. She could do it and she'd have my parents there to help her, but it would be lonely and hard.

I swung around and gave her a hug. "I'm so proud of you."

She squeezed me back. "Thank you, Jade. I hadn't realized how much I needed to hear that."

Aunt Allison beamed. "She's going to make a great alpha. Like you with Bevin and José, many of the kids, and several of the younger pack members, already go to her with their problems. Pebble, we're all proud of you."

Pebble blinked, as if trying to hold back tears.

We walked to the fence that separated the hiking trails from the pack's property. I needed a few minutes to rest before we headed back.

A strong kick from one of the three babies, and a cramp, probably a Braxton-Hicks, a fake contraction, had me groaning in pain. The real ones were at least a month off. A sliver of the tremor wiggled its way up to my head. I heard what sounded like a thunderous crash as a headache started.

"Two more days until Christmas. This decision to go on vacation was such a good one. I mean, I love the pack, but I need 'us' time." *Who said that?*

I gaped at Pebble and looked down at our clasped hands. *When did that happen?* "What? What do you mean you're going on vacation, or is this the vacation you mean?" *What is Pebble talking about?*

The world went watery, spinning around me. I reached for the gate, but everything spun.

"I know, I'm so excited to ski."

My free hand rubbed my forehead. "What do you mean 'ski?'"

Next to me, Pebble rubbed my back. "Jade? What are you talking about?" Stress filled her words.

I shook my head. "What are *you* talking about? A vacation? Skiing?"

Aunt Allison came up on my other side. "No one's said any of that." She sounded worried, too.

"Our flight leaves in an hour. Being at the airport is awful! Gods, I can't wait to be away from here."

That voice! I shut my eyes. Leaning on the fence, I lowered myself to the ground, then brought myself to my mental landscape. It was a place I'd created to help me communicate with my beasts. It appeared as a campsite with a log cabin, a small fire with logs to sit on, a lake in the background—and a screaming ghost caught within a cone of silence.

Panther, black sleek, and beautiful, stood near me, by the fire. Wolf, dubbed the black devil in high school, was nearby, on my other side. Swan, who usually swam in the lake, flew above. All three were close, sensing my distress.

Everything my mind had created for this outdoor scene fit, connected in some way. The one thing that didn't belong in the outdoor landscape happened when Piper, an old ex-girlfriend, turned wolfy for the first time. Somehow, an image of her imprinted on me and left a ghost behind in my mind. It was usually locked away, barely visible or recognizable for what she was. Despite that, every now and again Bevin, the strongest of my alphas, had to reinforce her cell in my mind.

Over the years, as Piper had grown as a wolf, her connection to me had strengthened. The need to lock down her image had happened more frequently. When the imprint was free, like now, I could often hear what she said, sometimes know what she thought and felt. Depending on her actions, it could be very uncomfortable.

It was always awkward and distracting, and not because she was an ex. This much personal information that I couldn't filter out would be uncomfortable with anybody.

The only good thing I'd ever figured out was that Piper didn't know anything about it.

"Jade?!" Pebble shook my shoulder. "Jade? What's wrong?"

"Jade, dear, is there anything we can do?" Aunt Allison's concern felt like a child's blanket wrapping around me. Being a submissive, like Brooke, she helped to ground me, but, at the moment, it wasn't enough. I wasn't even sure Brooke would be sufficient.

Instead of answering either of them directly, I reached out for Pebble's hand and mentally pulled Pebble into my landscape. She'd been here before, but never when Piper was free. When Piper was locked down, she was almost invisible. Bevin had more power than most people knew, and when he stretched his ability, it was awesome.

"Whoa! That was trippy." Pebble walked around, reacquainting herself with the area. Her face lit up when she gazed at my majestic animals.

"I'm heading to the bathroom. Watch my stuff, 'k? I'll be back shortly."

Pebble's jaw dropped open and her head snapped up, shifting from Wolf to the ghost. "I heard that. Even though the ghost isn't moving, I heard all of that. It was Piper, right? Jade, what's going on?"

I sat on one of the logs around the fake fire. Pebble sat down next to me. My animals piled in around us, agitated by Piper's freedom. Panther placed her head in my lap, and Wolf leaned up against my back. Swan landed, waddling to stand between me and

Pebble. A melodious squawk announced her opinion on the situation.

"When Piper had her first shift, I helped José pull out her wolf. He was a new alpha and didn't know what to do. I was new to understanding what it meant to be epsilon, and no one knows the extent of my abilities. I was connected to him mentally, telling him what Mom does."

I paused, remembering that day, the cool weather and Piper's excitement and fear. I trembled at the memory of what happened next. "After José commanded her to shift, an image of her stayed with me. Not being an alpha, I couldn't get rid of it. None of the alphas around me could exorcize her from my head either. José tried, Mom tried, hell, even Sarah tried. Over the years, we've just come up with other solutions, mainly to cover up the ghost and deal."

Pebble gazed at the ghost and shook her head. "Jade, I wish you'd've told me. This is awful. Whatever you're doing, it isn't working."

I clenched my jaw then relaxed snapping out, "What we're doing is our best."

Because Pebble had been so young at the time, she'd never been told the full story. As she got older, it never occurred to any of us to share my story outside of me and my alphas.

My sister's eyes narrowed. "In all these years, why haven't you ever told me?"

I could hear her hurt, and I huffed out a sigh. "You were my kid sister. It was above your pay-grade."

"Jade, like you, I'm different. I'm closer to my wolf than anyone else. No one else has survived being bitten at five. No one else has been a werewolf so long they don't remember *not* being dual-natured. Gods above, save me from all of you. I'm starting college in the fall, I'm about to take over the Wisconsin pack, and I'm your sister." I could hear the tears she wouldn't shed. "Please treat me better."

My heart hurt. I pulled her into a hug, easier here where my belly didn't weigh me down. "I'm sorry."

"Oh! That's our flight. Julez, this is it!"

With a low growl, I pushed away from Pebble. "We need to get back. If Bevin doesn't fix this, I'm going to go crazy. It used to be just the ghost, but if I have to hear everything she says, then I may literally need a padded room."

Pebble bumped her shoulder into mine. "Don't worry, I think that was part of the original Were House plan. I mean, the boys *do* know you're part of the pack, after all."

I snorted.

Her smile widened and warmth suffused me. I loved my sister. "Okay, Jade, I know you want Bevin to fix this, but can I try something? I may be able to help with the ghost. I have an idea."

"You think you can help? Hide the ghost?"

She nodded. "Yeah, or something more permanent."

Hope shot through me, but I suppressed it. Pebble was young, and many people had tried to take care of my ghost. "I mean, sitting here is good to ensure we make it back. If I don't rest between legs of the walk, I can't do anything. But, Pebble, realize this—everyone has tried to help, and everyone has failed. I don't want you to feel bad if this doesn't work." I bit my lip, hoping she'd understand my hesitation.

Pebble wrapped an arm around me. "I know. Mom, Sarah, José, Bevin ... you have so many people who love you. But they aren't me. They are all alphas, but I'm ... I don't know, I'm just different. Like you. Different."

"I know. Do your worst ... or best."

Pebble shut her eyes. There was a vibration in the air, and all my animals pushed in tighter. I realized Pebble's gray wolf had been hiding behind Panther, but she came up and nuzzled my hand, asking for a pat.

Suddenly, I felt strange tendrils of cool electricity flow through me. The feeling started to heat as my head buzzed. I curled my head to my knees, wrapping my hands around my ears, and breathed slowly, but roughly.

My body started to tremble. "Jade, are you okay?" Aunt Allison's voice floated over me like a cool breeze.

I couldn't answer, but I managed a small nod.

The stereo sound of Pebble mumbling next to me and within my mental landscape was eerie. The feeling of a knife down my spine cut off all other thoughts. I whimpered.

Then ... nothing. There was a moment that sound and feeling seemed to vanish.

After a beat of this seeming void, in my mindscape, a cool breeze blew across my hands which still covered my face. Pebble rubbed my back. "It's okay, Jade. Look."

I heard a chorus of two wolves howling and Panther chuffing. The chorus didn't sound unhappy.

It was enough.

I finally uncurled, my muscles tight and cramped as if I'd fought nine rounds with a professional boxer. My animals all stood near me, along with Pebble's wolf. Panther rubbed against my shoulder. A low grumble from her gut sounded suspiciously like a purr. Wolf bounced on her front paws and Pebble's wolf danced. Swan took to the air, flying in circles. I could feel their joy.

Looking around my landscape, I saw Pebble standing near the small fire, a few inches from me, with a tentative smile on her face. "Are you okay?"

Beyond Pebble should've been the ghost, but there was … nothing. An open area that led to the wooded background. I stood and turned in a circle. Nothing. I closed my eyes but felt … nothing. "She's gone?"

Pebble's face lit. "She's gone."

"Oh my gods!" I flew to my sister and squeezed her, tears pricking my eyes. Almost a third of my life I'd dealt with a ghost in my head, and my genius of a sister finally figured out how to help me. "You are amazing! What did you do?"

Pebble shrugged. "I sent her home. I don't know how to describe it. There was a connection I could see that needed to be resolved. So," her face scrunched up, "she's gone now."

Once out of the mindscape, and standing, a feat unto itself, I told Aunt Allison what had happened. "Pebble, that's fantastic!" She threw her arms around my sister. "I knew Hazel made the right choice with you being the next alpha. You're kind, compassionate, and as clever as they come! I'm so proud of you."

A few minutes later, we went back to Were House. The total distance wasn't far, but after everything that had happened, it stretched my abilities. I curled into my recliner chair with tea, snacks, and a book. I refused to nap; I was too happy.

As soon as I saw Bevin, José, and Sarah, I was thrilled to tell them what Pebble had done. They each wanted to see for themselves. Not feeling strong enough to have a full alpha party in my mindscape, I brought them in separately. They each whooped with pride.

With so much mental activity to drain my reserves, Oscar made sure to keep the chocolate shakes coming. We ordered Pebble's favorite food, Thai, while Oscar and Aunt Allison baked a celebratory cake.

The next morning, José and Bevin joined me on my walk. It may have been to support me, more likely to have a few minutes of peace to recharge. It was Christmas Eve, and the house was full to bursting.

Bevin had been up when I'd made it out for breakfast, coming in from his morning torture, the daily exercises Owen individualized for each pack member. It was maybe the one benefit of being pregnant. No torture for me. It was difficult enough getting out of bed.

Owen *did* give me a few suggestions, but he was too afraid of my wrath and Sarah's disapproval to push me. I figured after the walk I might swim. Those were it for my 'to dos.'

By the end of the walk, I wanted to collapse. It was hard to put one foot in front of the other and focus on the conversation. Inside the house, I bee-lined to my favorite nesting spot, but the front door burst open, and Owen blew in before I made it.

"Sis! You're up. Don't sit."

I snarled at him. "It's official. You have a death wish."

His smile lit up the room, brighter than the Christmas lights. He flew across the room to me and slid his arm under mine. "Come on, Mamacita, we have guests."

"More guests? Gah! I just want to sit. Anyone visiting can come to me on my throne."

"Your blanket nest? Probably, but humor me."

Before I could snap back, Mom and Dad, followed by Uncle Jackson, walked through the door. With Owen's help, I almost moved at normal human speed to reach them. It was a Christmas present to see them, and my happiness overshadowed the throbbing in my feet.

Mom and Dad engulfed me in a huge hug. Then Uncle Jackson. My face hurt from smiling. "You made it!" I laughed. "No one told me you were arriving today." I lightly punched Owen, who obviously had known.

Mom hugged me again. "You have a lot on your mind. You look ready to pop, dear. How many do you have in there, a dozen?"

From the dining room, Bevin groused, "Don't you dare answer that question. You know the rules. You speak, you'll be dumped in the pool."

From the other side of my parents, Sarah laughed. "His threat is different every time."

"Doesn't make it any less real," he mumbled. Despite the words, a citrusy scent of humor came from the dining room. He was serious about not wanting to know anything, but he was also having fun.

I kept my face blank as I nodded. "You guessed it—an even dozen. By February, we'll have a track team."

José snorted. "Or need one to keep up with them."

Dad swung his arm around me. "That's my girl. Now, let's get you to a seat before you collapse. Is the dining room okay? We'd like to catch up."

Chapter 7 - A Three-Ring Circus
Bevin

I sat by the pool while Jade swam. Her parents had been here for a few hours, and they'd met Garrett. They were heading with Owen to take him to the airport so he could return home for Christmas. There was no reason he couldn't be with his family for the holidays. Garrett said he'd return in January for the full moon.

Jade needed some downtime, so for now, I was the only one with her. Others may join her soon. This close to Christmas, many of the pack were in town shopping, some were lounging inside. Most days Jade wanted to do something. The fact that she didn't want to leave Were House was more worrisome than anything I'd heard. She'd find any excuse to convince people to get ice cream. It was the main reason Allison and I decided to stay behind.

Jade swam laps, but not very fast. Mostly she floated. I think the alleviation of weight from her body was what she wanted more than exercise.

A cool splash of water hit my face. "Hey, you should join me in here, not mope out there. The baby—or could it be more? You'll never know!" She cackled. "Anyway, they're very active. I bet they could knock you out with one of their kicks right now."

With a grin, I leapt in. Sure enough, with my hand on her side, one of the kiddos—since at this point I knew it wasn't just one—kicked or punched my hand. I laughed and she smiled at my enjoyment. After a moment, she winked and went back to her exercise, one of the few she could do comfortably.

A quarter of an hour later, at the far end of the pool, she popped her head up again. "Want to join me in laps? We could race."

"Hmm, Tempting. But no, you 'swim.'" I quoted the word with my fingers then leapt away from a larger splash from the pool. "I'm enjoying relaxing here."

"Jerk. You lug around a pack day in and day out and see how fast *you* move."

I smiled at her. "I'm sure I will, but hopefully not until January. Once the pups, as you call them, are out, you can take time off, and I'll love them, and squeeze them, and—"

"We are *not* naming any of the pups 'George.'"

Laughter bubbled out of me. "You know, it's an excellent name. Not very common anymore. I think you're missing out on name gold here."

Her eyes narrowed. "No." Then she floated towards the far end of the pool on her back.

I watched her expressions. She made faces as the kiddos did things. A wince, a shudder, a small jerk, a smile. I had no idea what the babies were doing, but I could almost write a story based on her impressions.

A peace relaxed her as she floated back towards me. I knew it wouldn't last, but it was nice that she had a few moments of downtime. She flutter-kicked her feet as she came back towards me.

She continued to do her laps, and I imagined what animals our future kids may have. I kept snapping at everyone that I didn't want to know how many pups she carried because I wanted it to be a surprise. I don't know why; I guess it was about having something unknown. Despite that, like any future dad ... *dad!!!* ... I was curious. *Could any of them be a double or even a double with a swan like her? Is that even a thing?*

With Jade's epsilon ability, she'd opened up a whole new world of magic to us. If I told her she was magic, she'd probably try to hit me. She was cute when she thought she could take one of us down, even with her three animals. She was fierce, and against anyone not pack, and not trained by Owen, I'd put money on her, but her magic ... it boggled my mind. I wasn't sure how she stayed grounded with everything that had happened to her and everything she could do.

She flipped in the shallow end and winced. She turned, grabbed her side, and grunted.

"Jade, are you okay?" I was on my feet at the side of the pool.

"I ... ah."

"Jade?" I dropped to my knees, unconcerned that I fell onto cement. "Talk to me, are you okay?"

Her eyes flashed and she held her stomach. "Bevin, it hurts." She gasped, her black curls plastered down her back and on her face. Between a few strands, her green eyes were the size of dinner plates. She looked desperate.

Heart in the back of my throat, I leapt into the water, picked her up, and carried her out. "Where?"

She curled into me and moaned. She started to shake. "Let me breathe through this one, it won't be long ... I don't think—"

Her body stiffened and then trembled. She whimpered as I stood next to the pool holding her, rocking her like a child. "I wish I could take this pain away from you." But there was nothing I could do but hold her.

As quickly as it started, it stopped. Her breathing evened out and her body relaxed. "Put me down, Bev. Let me walk. Oh, and find me a towel." She stopped and gave me a small smile. "Gods, I'm sorry. I'm being bossy."

I shook my head. "Be bossy. I'm sorry you're in so much pain. Anything else you need?" I wrapped her in a large beach towel that had been draped over a pool chair.

She tugged the ends closed, then gazed up at me. She looked young and lost. "Find Aunt Allison. I need you both with me. I can't do this alone."

I hugged her. "I'm with you to the end. You know that."

Oh, my gods, the babies!

I sent a quick text to Allison and José, `Pool, contractions, come quick.` I didn't think I could manage more.

Within fifteen minutes, Allison, Pebble, Brooke, José, and Alex were all out in the back with us, by the pool. Her contractions were steady, but not close enough together that Allison was worried. We decided to bring out Settlers of Catan to play as a distraction.

Despite being in labor, Jade won the first game. By the time it was done, her parents were back with Owen and Sarah.

We offered a second round, but the pain was obvious, so she moved to her bed. She closed her eyes and was silent for a few minutes. We all knew that meant she was talking with her animals.

Her ability to communicate with her beasts was a marvel. Of all her epsilon skills, that may have been the one I envied most. You'd think as alpha it would be her ability to talk with anyone in the pack at just about any distance, but no. I would have loved to be able to speak with my wolf. Thank him for everything he's done for me, for us as a pack. For everything.

Not only could she speak with her animals, she had a full mental landscape. A mini, made-up campground where her animals lived. The few times I'd been there, I'd come closer to communicating with my wolf than any other time. I'd tried to meditate to create my own, but nothing I did worked.

She opened her eyes. "Panther said she'd help. I think ... *think*, mind you, I'm about to evict some rugrats."

She'd been having some contractions, her body wracked with pain, for a few hours. I hoped it was almost done. I knew women could go much longer, but if her animals could help ...

Brooke sat behind her, supporting her. I sat on one side of the bed, holding her hand, José on the other. She had the full complement of pack touch to pull on.

Allison was there to deliver the babies. Alex was there to help. Like Alex, Allison was a vet by practice and didn't love being a human doctor, but this was one of the things she enjoyed: bringing babies into the world. I could've helped, but I knew Jade needed me beside her.

Allison sighed. "It looks like this still may take some time. I know you're ready to get these babies out right now, but you may have an hour or so."

Jade snarled. "I'm glad there's more than one, because I think this is it. Never again."

Allison chuckled. "You say that now, but you may change your mind later. You never know."

Brooke snorted. "Or not. I'm not pushing for more kids."

Jade leaned into Brooke with a satisfied smile before another contraction overtook her.

Pebble, sitting in a seat on the far side of the room, gazed at them, her focus off. It was a look that said it could be her or her wolf. "Brooke, tell me a story."

For a second, I thought she'd ignore the request, but then Brooke narrowed her eyes. "What type of story?"

"Tell me about how you and Jade went from enemies to engaged."

Chapter 8 - A Bedtime Story
Brooke

I held Jade to me. Her body shook with another contraction. In my soul, I could feel the string of pain sizzle through her. On either side of Jade, Bevin and José held back their joy and wonder, only showing her their stoic concern for her pain.

Watching the movement in her stomach, all I could think was: I never want to have kids.

How much longer will this take? I want Jade to be out of pain.

Allison sighed. "It looks like this still may take some time. I know you're ready to get these babies out right now, but you may have an hour or so."

Pebble, sitting in a seat on the far side of the room, gazed at me, her focus off, as if in a trance. *Is she talking with her wolf?* "Brooke, tell me a story."

Gods above, I'm so focused on Jade and her condition. One of my brows lifted habitually. Then I realized this was bigger than me ... I narrowed my eyes. "What type of story?"

"Tell me about how you and Jade went from enemies to engaged."

My belly tightened. Before I could say anything, Jade chuckled. "It started six years ago."

I growled low in my gut. "Love, your sister asked me, so let me tell the story while you have the babies. Maybe I can distract you for a few moments."

She sighed. "Very well, when do *you* think it started?"

"Well, she asked about enemies, and I think we should start there."

Jade groaned. "I don't want to talk about high school, not now."

I smiled. "Let me talk, love."

A vibration against my chest from Jade was the only reaction I got.

"I'd always played a role in high school. My family was pretty awful, so I stuck with my friends and pushed everyone else away. I liked Owen; he was fun, but he was way too close with his family." Everyone in the room snickered with me. Now, I knew why Owen would have never walked away from his pack.

Pebble tilted her head. "Wait, are you bisexual or did my brother turn you gay?"

I barked out a laugh. "Oh, Owen definitely turned me gay. Without a doubt." Once everyone stopped snickering, I continued. "In college, I finally learned to be myself. I dated different people and started figuring out what and who I wanted to be. When I saw Jade in Las Vegas, she'd just graduated high school. If we hadn't had a history, if she wasn't there with Owen and José, if she didn't mostly hate me ... who knows. Then we were taken and the whole werewolf thing happened."

Jade scoffed. "Hadn't officially graduated high school. I was a junior and hadn't done early graduation yet."

Everyone in the room groaned. "Love, let me talk. That's a detail that isn't pertinent to the story. You started college with Bev the next year, so, no more high school, good enough for government work, and you do work for the government some of the time."

José threw back his head and laughed. "You gloss over the kidnapping as if it were nothing. You gave all of us such hell for that 'whole werewolf thing.' Jade was assigned your teacher, and you tweaked her at every turn."

"Well, yeah. I was starting to like her. She didn't like me, and she's fun to tease. Poking at little Ms. Perfect is always a joy."

Bevin narrowed his eyes at me. "Was fun to tease or *is* fun to tease?"

I shrugged. "Yes?"

"Can she talk? You're giving her as much hassle as you joke she gives Jade," Pebble complained.

I winked at her. "As cool as I could play it, my wolf, my inner soul, was always obvious."

Jade's head dropped back. "You know, now that you mention it, I feel a bit oblivious."

Bevin and José both laughed this time. Bevin shook his head. "The more animals you collected, Jade, the more likely you've been to ignore everything. The idea of you ignoring things that are right in front of you ... it's not surprising."

I moved my hands to Jade's shoulders and massaged as her body trembled with another contraction. "You've gotten better, love, but you do tend to ignore the world around you."

"You were telling a story, not having a Jade intervention," she groused. "So, I missed the obvious, I just don't understand how we went from Las Vegas to five years later." Her face scrunched up as she gazed at me. "You play the long game."

"Well, I mean, there were times in there I was just angry, and you frustrated me. You kept picking dates who were all wrong for you."

Alex snorted. "I just don't know how everyone didn't know you and your wolf were half-mated to Jade from the start. That was the first thing I noticed about you."

"Yeah, and that's why one of the first things I said to you was a threat."

Alex smiled at me. "I've always liked you."

I chuckled. "Right back at ya."

Pebble grumbled, "Story, please."

I sighed. "Fine. Throughout Jade's college years, once I moved here, I didn't want to get in the way of her own discovery. She made some awful decisions and some interesting ones. I tried to slowly move our original high school antagonistic relationship into something cordial. It started with supporting her. Then, once she was single and ready, I finally bit the bullet and made my move."

Jade wiggled back into me. "This is the part of the story I know better."

I patted her head. "Yes, love. This is where you've finally caught up. I would sneak flowers into her room, but since her nose can scent anything, she knew it had been me. Then I left chocolate. I finally worked up to asking her out to dinner."

Pebble sat up. "How? You didn't just go up to her and say, 'let's try out a new restaurant,' right? I think I heard about it."

This was one of my favorite memories, and not only because Jade said yes. "I found a dress that I knew would look fantastic on her. Now, she'd accepted the flowers and chocolate without a word, just a few awkward looks—you know the ones. So, the next time I snuck into her room, I laid the dress out on her bed with a note. *Let's test this dress out Friday night.*"

Jade had a contraction, her whole body tensing. She breathed loudly and rhythmically. After a minute she said, "That was a good date. We should go there on New Year's. Just us."

I slid my arms around her. "Oh, yeah! This whole thing means we can do that, doesn't it? We can go on a non-pregnant date night. No alcohol, but a more comfortable evening."

José smiled at me. "I think you two having a date night sounds great, as long as you're back for sleeping bags and movies at midnight. A tradition is a tradition."

Pebble leaned back. "So that's the story. And the rest is history?"

"And the rest is history," Jade said with a content sigh, melting into me. I loved the feel of her against me, even when I threatened her in the early hours of the morning.

Warmth filled me. "Yep, and the rest is history."

José looked across Jade to Bevin. "Look at us, we have our family. Two dads, two moms, and a pack of pups on the way." He winked at me. "Wanna know how many, Bev?"

Bevin snarled. "Do not start with me. We have a few more hours of mystery. Our very own Christmas presents."

I squeezed Jade. "Don't take until Christmas. These kids deserve a day for gifts separate from a national holiday."

She laughed. "Ow, ow, ow, another contraction. Don't make me laugh."

It took another hour or so, but the babies were determined to come on Christmas Eve.

The delivery took time and sounded painful. I tried to massage Jade as best I could. Me and the boys all tried. I knew Jade's animals were helping as well, though I wasn't sure what they did.

After some time, Allison looked up with a giant smile. "It's a girl." She held the first baby up. Bright blue eyes, a mirror to Bevin's, gazed at him. The boys had promised Jade she could name the babies, but I'd heard them discuss hoping for a girl with a Hispanic name. Jade and I had talked about it as well.

Jade's face brightened and she looked back and forth between the boys. "Bevin, José, meet Esperanza."

Warmth erupted in me as I watched the joy in José's and Bevin's faces.

A second baby came out, a boy with dark brown hair and brown eyes. He looked serious and as beautiful as any baby I could ever imagine.

Jade nodded as she trembled. "Binium."

José took their son ... our son.

Jade wasn't done. She was still pushing. I put my mouth to her ear so only she could hear. "One more, love. You can do it."

It took a couple of minutes for a dark-haired girl with green eyes to be presented to us. Jade slumped, breathing hard. "Calista, the last one will be named Calista."

For the next bit of time, Jade nursed the three babies. Once satiated, they each fell asleep. Gazing at Jade and the three lives strewn in the bed around her, it occurred to me just how insane our life was about to get.

Chapter 9 - Christmas Morning
Jade

I woke up ... again. But I didn't care. I could move. I leapt up and wanted to skip to the loo but didn't want to wake anyone up. We'd set up a bunch of mattresses on the floor of the babies' room, two queen sized mattresses with a twin in between. Brook and I slept in one, Bevin and José slept in the other, and the three babies were swaddled in between.

We weren't sure how long we planned on keeping the room set up like this, but we knew this allowed for anyone to rock a pup when one woke up and kept the odds in favor of the adults.

As quietly as I could, I navigated out of the room and into mine and Brooke's. I took a quick shower, marveling at how easy it was to move, then went into my closet and just stared at my clothes. I had no idea what to wear. I finally chose a pajama set Pebble had given me years ago with geese on it. Elastic was a necessity.

Within a blink of my eyes, I sat in the dining room. I forgot how quickly I could move without a large belly. I giggled in glee as Oscar placed a coffee in front of me. I swooned. It had been so long since I'd had coffee. It felt like I should savor it. I picked it up, then slowly relished my first sip since ... I couldn't even remember. I'd tried not to hyper focus on my first love. *Wait, chocolate, shakes ... family ... hmmm maybe fourth love.*

"Child, I know it's Christmas, but you're worrying me."

How could I forget?

"Merry Christmas, Oscar! Wait, why am I worrying you?"

He sat down next to me with his own coffee and two plates of sausage rolls. "You're groaning and moaning over that coffee." He shook his head. "Merry Christmas. We only have a few minutes before the hordes descend."

"I can't believe the kids aren't down here tearing into their stockings already."

He checked his watch. "It's not six. Rules, child, rules."

Owen and Sarah joined us. Sarah's smile was larger than my brother's. "You look so animated, Jade. It's about time. Want to take a run with me later this afternoon?"

Oscar slipped away, returning with coffee for each of us. Then a full platter with sausage rolls, eggs, and bacon. The sideboard had plates.

I leaned back. "Maybe. I don't know what I can do yet, but maybe you, me, and Brooke can take my body out for a test run."

Owen scoffed. "What? You'd leave me out?"

"You'll be busy with your nieces and nephew."

His face glowed. "You know, those three kids are awfully cute. The first kids born in Were House." He turned and winked at Sarah. "Not the last, though."

She shook her head. "Yes, I know you want kids."

"When are you thinking?" I knew they'd been discussing ever since I'd started showing.

Sarah shrugged. "I thought summer."

My jaw dropped. "You're pregnant."

Owen squealed, looking back and forth between us. "We can tell people now?"

One of Sarah's shoulders shrugged. "We're through the first trimester, why not?"

"Best gift!" He started dancing in his seat.

Next to me, Oscar snorted. "This house is going to be insane. At least four kiddos?"

I snapped my head to Sarah. "Do you want to know?"

Owen shook his head. "No!" at the same time Sarah held out her hand. "Of course!"

Before Owen could stop me, I snatched the hand held out to me. Owen grabbed both our wrists and pulled our hands apart. "No! Say nothing. Did you have enough time? Of course, you had enough time. Gods, Jade, say nothing. Do you know?"

"I know you're babbling." I laughed at him.

Our parents sauntered in. Mom looked wide awake. Dad looked like a walking zombie.

"Mom, why did you drag Dad from bed? It's his vacation. Why didn't you let him sleep?"

Dad tried to glare at Mom, but it came out more like a confused stumble. They sat and Owen got up to grab them plates.

"It's Christmas and he has new grandbabies. He can suffer for a day."

He grunted, then gave a half smile to Oscar after he handed him a large mug of coffee.

Mom searched our faces. "Okay, what were you two fighting about this time? Aren't you two old enough to not fight? Every time I enter a room with you two it's something."

Sarah shook her head with a chuckle. "How do you know your kids are fighting?"

"It's something in their eyes. A mother always knows."

I scoffed. "Don't believe it, Sarah. She could hear us. She's always been able to hear us."

"That, too. Now fill me in."

Owen glared at me. His glare was much better than Dad's. "Sarah's pregnant and—"

"Oh! Congratulations, dear!" Mom interrupted. "That's fantastic. When are you due?"

Sarah leaned over for a hug. "Thanks. We're due this summer."

"Do you know how many pups you're having?"

Owen growled. "Not you, too."

Mom snorted. "Ah, and now I know what the fight was about. Does Jade know?"

Sarah shot me a look, and I slowly nodded. "Apparently she does, but Owen is like Bevin—hell-bent on being old fashioned and ignorant."

Dad bent over his coffee, appearing mostly asleep. "You want information. Knowledge is power."

"You too, Dad?" Owen whined. "I need Bevin, he'll be on my side."

I sat on the couch cuddling into Booke, Sarah sat on my other side. Owen had run around handing out gifts. He said he needed a break and had gone to the kitchen for some hot chocolate. *I hope he's getting enough for everyone.*

Sarah shook my arm. "Tell me now while he's distracted. One? Two? Will I be suffering like you with three? Do you know about their animals? Talk to me, Jade."

Pulled from my thoughts of hot chocolate, I gaped at her. "What? Oh! No, not three. Ten." I tried to keep a blank face.

After a second of sputtering, she punched my arm. "Jade! I'm serious."

I smiled wickedly. "Twins."

"I have hot chocolate. Clear the table."

Pebble moved to clear the table. I held Esperanza, Bevin had Binium, and José cuddled with Calista so we couldn't help. Sarah handed out the mugs with candy canes in them.

Owen sat. "Okay, I have a stack of Jade's gifts. They all look the same, so no one should be surprised. Mom."

Mom grabbed the package thrown to her. She ripped open the wrapping. "Let's see, a T-shirt with a complicated function. Under it reads, 'What's not to understand?'"

José narrowed his eyes. "That's the quadratic function, right?"

Pebble's jaw dropped. "I was told you couldn't do math."

He threw a pillow at her. "Alright, punk. I can kick you out of my house."

Dad opened his. "'I'm not responsible for what you understand, only for what I said.' Mom should wear this to her classes."

"I'd be reprimanded."

José opened his shirt. "'If you love someone, let them sleep.'"

Dad sighed. "How do I get that one?"

Bevin opened his. A man who looked vaguely like him with three kids that looked like miniatures of me, José, and him. "'Best Dad Ever!'" His eyes narrowed. "Jade! You were going to give me this? Before the babies were born?"

"Nope, I had a different shirt. I bought you two."

He leaned forward and reached out the hand that wasn't supporting Binium. "Really? Gimme."

"Nope, you can have that in May. I'm prepared for your birthday."

Pebble read, "'Leader of the Pack.'" It had cats running in all directions. Her eyes narrowed, "Did you know?"

I shook my head. "No, that's just really random."

Owen opened his. Across the top it read: *Give me twenty!* Below there were two boxes, one with a twenty-dollar bill, the other a person doing a push up. He rolled, literally.

Sarah's shirt was a stylized top with a black panther.

For Brooke, I got a dress. Sarah helped me pick it out, but it would work for our New Year's Eve date.

She leaned over and gave me a soft kiss. "It's beautiful and thank you for not picking it out yourself."

Then there was Oscar. He snarled at me when he saw I'd gotten him a gift. He and his wife were planning on going to his son's place, but I caught him before he left. His was an apron with a chef's knife printed on it. It read: *Test me, I know how to use it!*

I got up to stretch. Sarah took Esperanza from me. "So, we're done?"

Dad grumbled. "When do I get a grandbaby? I flew all the way from Wisconsin, and—"

Owen and Pebble rolled their eyes and sing-songed with Dad, "Boy are my arms tired!"

He waggled his eyebrows at them. He held his hands out to Bevin with narrowed eyes. "Give, boy!"

Bevin smiled wide and handed Binium over. Not wanting to upset the grandparents, Sarah handed Esperanza to Mom.

I gazed at my family and a warmth filled me. This was the best gift I could have asked for. Three healthy pups. Happy parents, both mine, and for the babies. Everyone was healthy and safe. Next to me, Brooke stood. Being a submissive, she could feel my emotions, and probably knew the cause. She wrapped her arms around me and gave me a squeeze.

Pebble jumped to her feet. "No, not yet. You have one more gift, too. My gift!"

One of my brows rose. "Oh? Owen?"

He winked at me. "Huh, must have missed it. Here you go, sis."

I narrowed my eyes. I could never trust my family. The box was big, but I unwrapped it. Inside was a brand-new set of goose pajamas, with a huge image of an attacking goose on the shirt. Smaller versions of that image were on the pants. As I dug into the box, there were smaller onesie and pant versions of the pajamas for the kids.

We'd be able to wear matching goose pajamas. I pulled up my gape-mouthed, shocked face from the gift to see everyone in my family's joyous faces.

Merry Christmas!

Pebble's story to come ...

Pack Present

Thank you for reading Jade Stone Chronicles!

Please leave a review online.

Check out my website to find all the links to my socials and

find information on my next series!

Coming up:

- Pebble's Story

- A new series about a phoenix shifter!

Dedication

I want to thank all the readers for making my first effort at writing feel like coming home. I appreciate all the warm words of encouragement you have given me. I hope you will enjoy any future book and series I write.

Huckleberry Rahr is a mathematics instructor at the University of Wisconsin-Whitewater. She spent many years teaching math around the Midwest and in Papua New Guinea with the Peace Corps. Her parents instilled a love of reading from a young age.

She grew up with lesbian moms who had a huge collection of women authors with heroines as the protagonist. Her favorite genre was fantasy and science fiction, that is, until she discovered urban fantasy. What her mom's library lacked were books with characters that looked like her family: diversity in background, gender identity, and sexuality. She decided if she couldn't find that series, then she would write it.